Hairy Maclary's Bone

Other TRICYCLE PRESS books by Lynley Dodd

Hairy Maclary from Donaldson's Dairy
Hairy Maclary Scattercat
Hairy Maclary's Rumpus at the Vet
Hairy Maclary and Zachary Quack
Hairy Maclary's Showbusiness
Hairy Maclary's Caterwaul Caper

Slinky Malinki
Slinky Malinki Catflaps
Slinky Malinki, Open the Door

Tricycle Press and the Tricycle Press colophon are registered trademarks
of Random House, Inc.

Library of Congress Cataloging-in-Publication Data
Dodd, Lynley.
Hairy Maclary's bone / Lynley Dodd.
p. cm.
Summary: A small black dog uses a series of slick maneuvers
to protect his bone
[1. Dogs—Fiction. 2. Bones—Fiction. 3. Stories in rhyme.] I. Title.
PZ8.3.D637 Hal 2001b
[E]—dc21
2001027611
ISBN 978-1-58246-060-4

Printed in China

6 7 8 9 10 11 — 16 15 14 13 12 11

First Tricycle Press Edition

Hairy Maclary's Bone

Lynley Dodd

TRICYCLE PRESS
Berkeley

Down in the town
by the butcher's shop door,
sat Hairy Maclary
from Donaldson's Dairy.

Out of the door
came Samuel Stone.
He gave Hairy Maclary
his tastiest
bone.

Then off up the street
on scurrying feet,
on his way to the dairy
went Hairy Maclary.

And chasing him home,
with their eyes on the bone,
went Hercules Morse,
Bottomley Potts,
Muffin McLay,
Bitzer Maloney
and Schnitzel von Krumm
with the very low tum.

Hungrily sniffing
and licking their chops,
they followed him up
past the school and the shops.

They came to the sign
selling Sutherland's Sauce.
Through they all went —

except Hercules Morse.

They came to a hedge
along Waterloo Way.
Under they went —

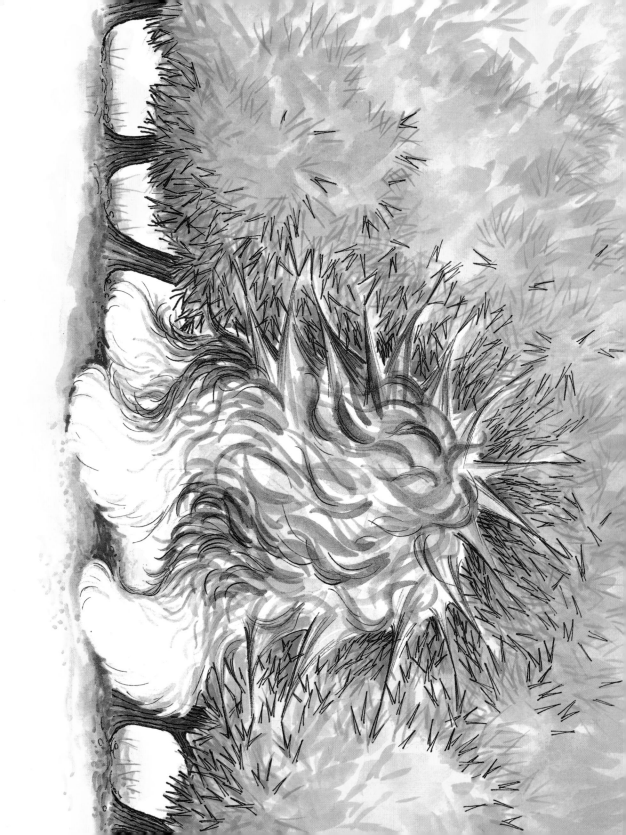

except Muffin McLay.

They came to a yard
full of dinghies and yachts.
Round they all went —

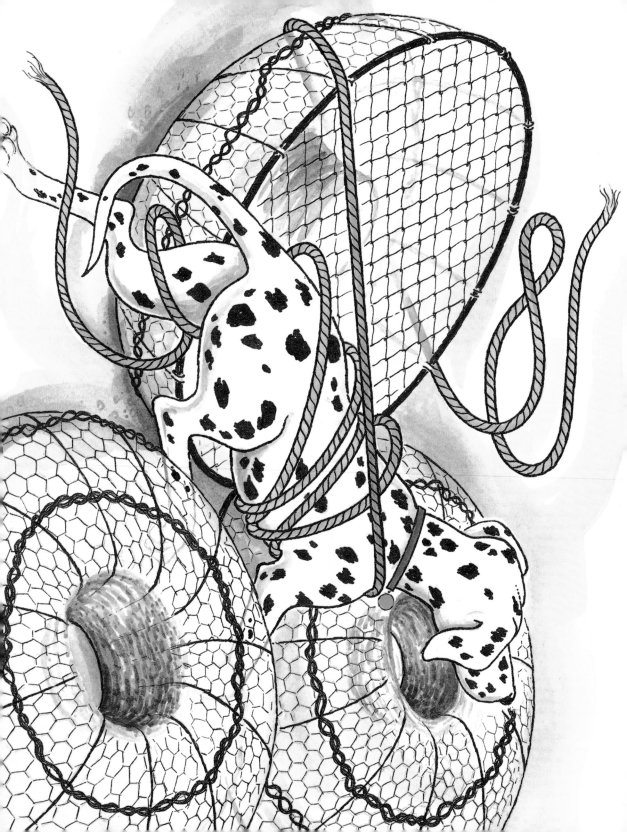

except Bottomley Potts.

They came to a building site,
cluttered and stony.
Over they went —

except Bitzer Maloney.

They came to a wall
by the house of Miss Plum.
One of them jumped —

but not Schnitzel von Krumm.

So at last he was free
to go home on his own,
Hairy Maclary
with ALL of his
bone.